GABBY GIVES BACK

Written by Crystal Senter-Brown
Illustrated by Janice Treece-Senter

ISBN: 978-1523254224

Gabby Girl Media

© 2016 Crystal Senter-Brown, Janice Treece-Senter

For exclusive content or to join the author's mailing list, visit www.crystalsenterbrown.com.

For school appearances, speaking engagements and more, email the author at gabbygirlmedia@gmail.com.

Download free worksheets, coloring pages and more at www.gabbygivesback.com.

For Aaliyah Kymani.

HI THERE! My name is Gabby! What is your name?

_____

My Name Is

**TODAY IS SATURDAY AND
DADDY MADE PANCAKES TO EAT!
WHAT IS *YOUR* FAVORITE BREAKFAST TREAT?**

AFTER WE EAT,
DADDY SAYS:
"I'M GOING TO
VOLUNTEER TO HELP
THOSE IN NEED.
WOULD YOU
LIKE TO GO, GABBY?"
AND I SAID
"YES, PLEASE!"

AS WE LEAVE THE HOUSE, SNOW BEGINS TO FALL.
I LOVE SPENDING TIME WITH DADDY,
ESPECIALLY WHEN WE GO FOR WALKS!

MAGGIE'S PLACE

WHEN WE ARRIVE, I SEE THE WORDS
"MAGGIE'S PLACE" ON THE SIGN.
THERE ARE LOTS OF PEOPLE
WAITING IN LINE.

MAGGIE GIVES US AN APRON
AND A HAIRNET TO WEAR,
SHE THANKS US FOR TAKING
THE TIME TO SHOW
HOW MUCH WE CARE.

DADDY HELPS BY SERVING
FOOD TO THE MANY PEOPLE
WAITING IN LINE. SINCE I AM
TOO YOUNG TO SERVE,
I SAY A BIG "HELLO"
TO EACH PERSON
AS THEY PASS BY!

WHEN WE ARE ALL DONE,
WE WAVE GOODBYE
TO EVERYONE!

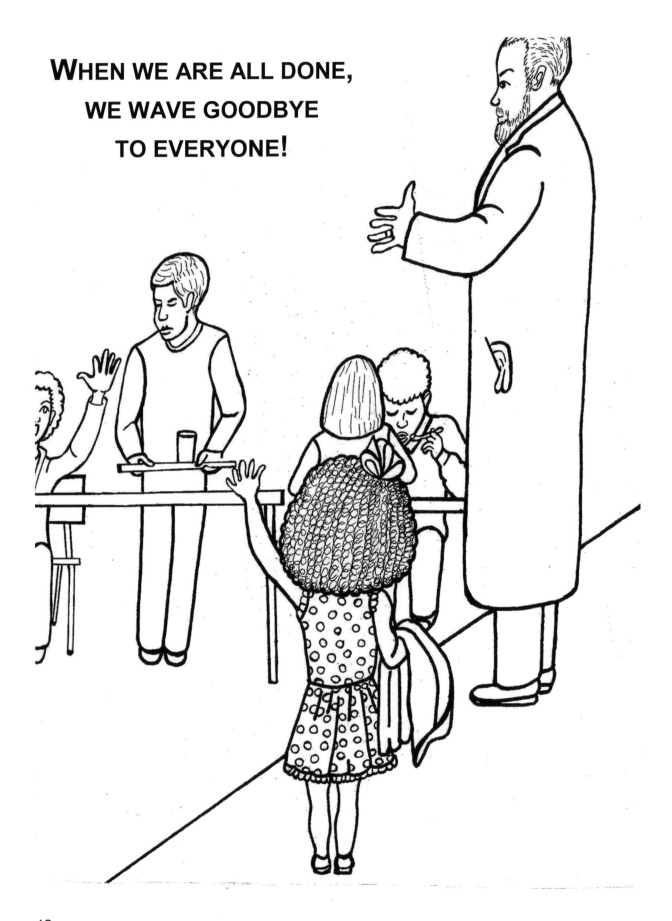

As we walk home, I tell Daddy "I would like to help, too!" He asks what I would like to do.

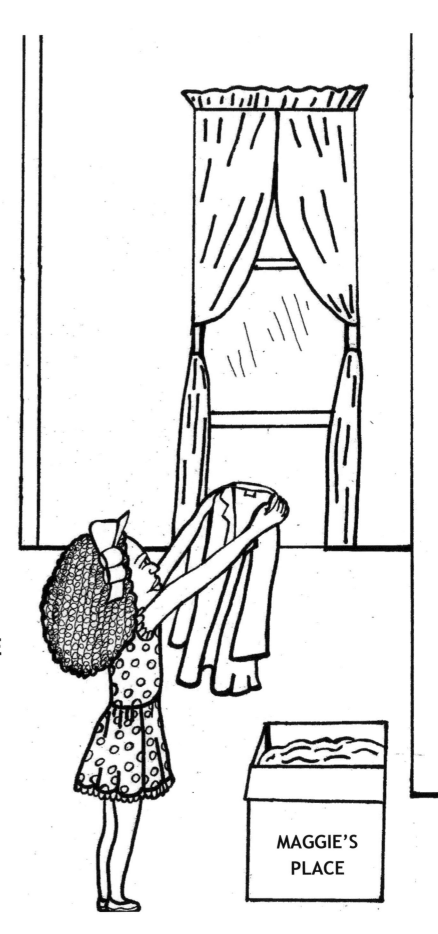

I TELL DADDY
"I WOULD LIKE TO GIVE
AWAY MY COATS THAT
NO LONGER FIT."
HE SAYS:
"GREAT IDEA!
LET'S GET TO IT!"

MAGGIE'S PLACE

MAMA SAYS SHE WOULD LIKE TO HELP
BY DONATING FOOD FROM OUR PANTRY.
SO WE CHOOSE SOME PASTA,
RICE, CORN, AND GREEN BEANS.

MAMA AND DADDY
ALSO LOOK THROUGH
THEIR CLOSET TO FIND
SOME CLOTHES FOR
US TO BRING,
THEN WE FIND A BIG
BOX TO HOLD
EVERYTHING.

MAGGIE'S
PLACE

**ONCE WE WERE DONE COLLECTING OUR ITEMS,
I DIDN'T WANT TO WAIT,
SO THAT AFTERNOON WE WENT BACK
TO MAGGIE'S PLACE!**

MAGGIE LOOKED THROUGH OUR DONATIONS, WHICH TOOK HER A LITTLE WHILE, "YOU ARE VERY GENEROUS!" SHE SAID WITH A BIG SMILE.

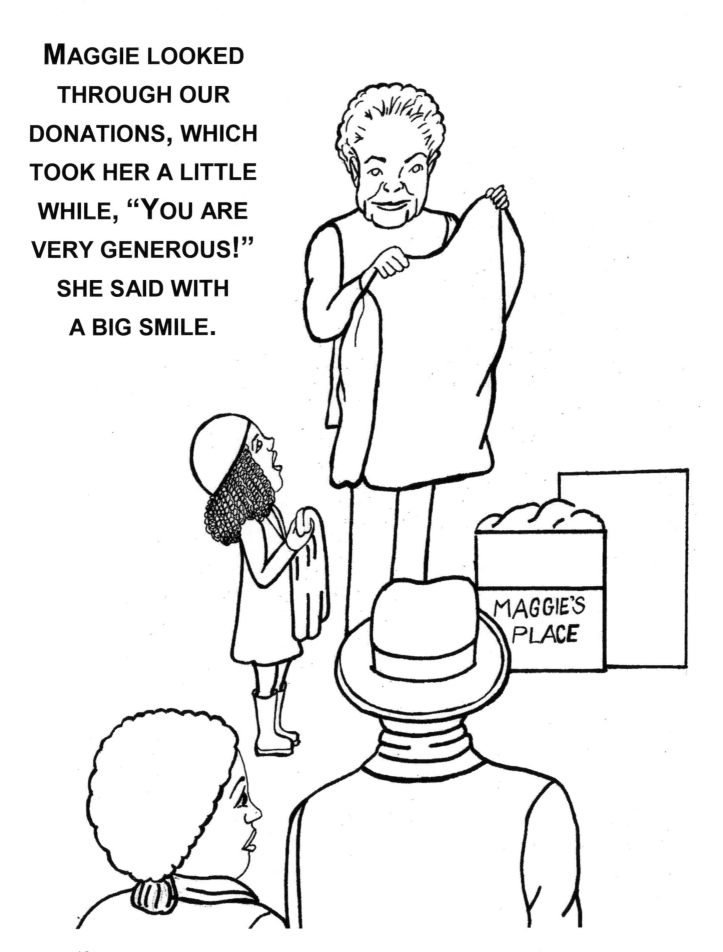

MAGGIE SAID THERE WAS A LITTLE GIRL WHO NEEDED A COAT TO KEEP HER WARM IN THE WINTER. SO I PULLED OUT THE COAT I BROUGHT WITH ME AND I WONDERED "WILL IT FIT HER?"

MAGGIE'S PLACE

IT FIT! THE LITTLE GIRL WAS VERY HAPPY.
THAT MADE ME HAPPY, TOO.

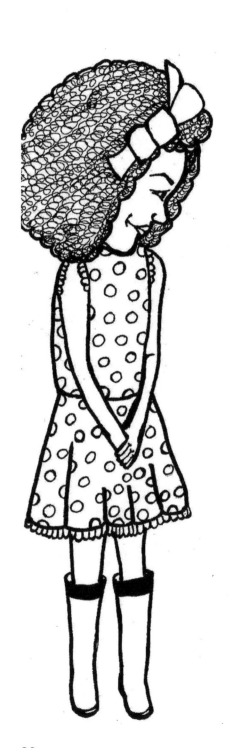

I LOVE TO HELP OTHERS- HOW ABOUT **YOU**?

ACTIVITIES

I can help others in my community by:

WORD SCRAMBLE

1. WNSO _____

2. GBABY _____

3. YDDDA _____

4. GGVNII _____

5. RESETLH _____

6. MSLNIG _____

7. EEPULLH _____

8. ISRENGV _____

9. HIRNGSA _____

10.   RMWA _____

WORDS:
- ☐ *WARM*
- ☐ *SHARING*
- ☐ *SERVING*
- ☐ *HELPFUL*
- ☐ *SMILING*
- ☐ *SHELTER*
- ☐ *GIVING*
- ☐ *DADDY*
- ☐ *GABBY*
- ☐ *SNOW*

WORD SEARCH

```
F E E A T I N G G M O T V G Q
A P M Q N U N J B D B J N V L
H W O O I I S N O W F I Y D R
E K I K V P L V X Z V O W D T
L X H R G W A L K I N G O A U
L Q E C F A T D G O T X O D R
O S L O C D B N Y S B C O D O
T U P Z A L E B A H F U C Y Y
L V I O Q T E F Y E H A C D Y
N Q N X A I K A D L D H W Y Q
E S G N A U Q N T N S M L N
F P O G E F C L Y E S C A G M
R D A R F G X J Y R X C M M L
O M B X H E L P F U L E A J E
V V T T K S L K K W F M C C D
```

WORDS

GABBY	DADDY	SHELTER	BREAKFAST
MAMA	COAT	SNOW	WALKING
HELPING	FOOD	EATING	SERVING
DONATE	BOX	CLEAN	HELLO
HELPFUL	MAGGIE	GIVING	

Draw a picture of what Gabby should do NEXT Saturday!

Complete the words. Which items should you donate to a shelter?

1. G___OVES

2. MI___ ___ENS

3. __AT

4. CA__ __ED G__ __D__

5. P__S__A

6. B__ __TS

7. C__ __TS

8. SH__ __S

9. B__ __NS

10. R__ __E

Books by Crystal Senter-Brown

But Now I See (Novel)
But You Have Such a Pretty Face (Poems)
Doubledutch (Poems)
Gabby Gives Back (Children's Book)
Gabby Saturday (Children's Book)
The Rhythm in Blue (Novel)

About the Author

Crystal Senter-Brown (**daughter**), has been featured in Redbook Magazine, Vibe Magazine and Essence Magazine and has been a performance poet and writer for most of her life. Born in Morristown, TN to a bass-playing Baptist preacher (Dad) and a visual artist (Mom), Crystal performed her first poem onstage at the age of six.

She is the author of five books: *But Now I See, But you have such a pretty face, Doubledutch, Gabby Saturday* and "*The Rhythm in Blue*". She is an adjunct professor and lives in New England with her husband Corey, son Adonte and a maniac puppy named Venus.

www.crystalsenterbrown.com.

About the Illustrator

Janice Treece- Senter (**mother**) was born in East Tennessee and has since lived throughout the Southeast as an Fine Artist and Childhood Artist Educational consultant. Self-taught, Janice has worked with of the best and brightest of fine artist throughout New England and the Southeast.

Her work has appeared internationally on the hit television show "Extreme Home Makeover" and she has received numerous awards for her art.

www.janicetreecesenter.com

Join the fun at

www.gabbygivesback.com!

• Find the answers to the

Gabby Gives Back activities

• Download coloring pages

• Send a message to Gabby

• Find a local shelter/ food pantry

in your community

• And more!

Made in the USA
Middletown, DE
20 March 2016